Too Many Peas in a Pod
by
Kevin Clinton

For you.

Too Many Peas in a Pod

Prologue:

Sebastian Preston was in the process of collecting his memoirs to build his resume. He had assembled all of his credentials together into one long reference table and he needed to incorporate some of the work mentioned in those credentials. With some of the few examples of what had sold through his agent, Cliff, he had known that the work would also need to be displayed in its best possible manner. So he was collecting the best of the best, which unfortunately was quite the rather stale task for quite the even staler materials.

He'd assembled his resume for the letters which he had

written, planning to send them out to any and all potential players for the lead role in his newest piece of writing, however, which itself had already been sold by that agent.

Cliff had long been with Sebastian, from his earliest of memoirs which were mostly fictional, although they were based off of personal witness of others and sometimes even based off Sebastian himself, as any writer's personal life goes into the work. Cliff knew that they both had something unique with which to mold between the two of them. Some aspects to the stories of course had to be changed in the course of the

work selling, sure, but only
when the companies choosing
to produce them into the
promotional visual-reels they
became would deem the changes
necessary – which was pretty
much all of the time. But
Sebastian didn't quite see it
the path on which he wanted
to settle. A company adapting
their promotional medium was
one thing but doing so no
matter the quality of the
originals just to make them
fit with what else might be
being promoted was too much.
Sebastian could never quite
settle knowing that no matter
how good the material was on
its own it simply didn't fit
into the world of all the
product-placement and trend-

following which film makers those days demanded.

Those days being of the first days anybody really saw anything of the internet was incidental. Piracy was easily committable with file-sharing and bootlegging websites, and so the only way for promotion companies to really make any money within the industry was to make the finished product something to behold with the setting of a grand theater. That meant the stories needed excuses made for effects and other special visual tactics, and Sebastian's stories never really fit that category. His stories were more reality-based.

Because of his struggle, Sebastian found it necessary

to call upon people within the industry since before all of these issues and make some pleas for commonality between players and roles before the promotional values even came about to the production teams and in fact before they even began production with one of his scripts. He chose the realest of his more recent stories and at the same time the one which would incite the most haunting potential in pursuit of visual effects for the production team to which it had just sold.

Carrie Rutherford was one of the many celebrities whom received Sebastian's call. He had used the medium of fan-mail to send his message so that he wouldn't get into any sort of financial obligations for soliciting where it was not allowed. Surely a great deal of authors contributed their ideas to fan-mail among those people of more obsessed nature. Sebastian however had faith in his credentials, and in that, the faith that some of his select celebrities would respond, at least one out of the few who even checked their fan-mail at all anyway. Whatever the odds were, he made sure they were better by sending to quite the large quantity of his ideal female leads and even those whom fit the criteria while *not* being ideal for his leads.

Carrie was busy wrapping up one of her many roles in feature productions, as the distraction of struggling so much at success had Sebastian typing out each letter one-by-one. None were specific to each celebrity except for the first greeting, but he had two versions of the letter. The first version praised the potential players each in the great promotional appearances of theirs and how they had all taken well advantage of what he had called the funny papers – or newsreels of the stars – and the other version contained praise for those respected individuals with an extraordinary ability to stay *away* from all of those funny papers.

The latter version was in Carrie's fan-mail box waiting for her, along with hundreds of other fan-mail boxes for other celebrities whom fit the category. She certainly was one very well-reserved individual, if not the type to particularly stand-out to him amongst her competition, but the point remains. Carrie was innocent as it pertained to her work morale. She often was cast supporting leads for her skills in fading out the image. She played the act of disappearing once each film was finished and never tried to hog the attention as it were. She was good at being the underdog, and that in her stood out to Sebastian when compared to her competition.

She lived in Hollywood so that she could keep in close contact with her own agencies and management studios from their home-bases even if the companies with whom she chose to work didn't film there in Hollywood. Her fan-mail box was also close to home this way. After-all, who holds fan-mail outside of the major industry cities? She enjoyed her reading it to herself in a neat little home, and so she lived in the big city. Her fans deserved it, and she even enjoyed sifting through the crazies.

Sebastian's stories along with his credentials struck Carrie oddly after she had received his correspondence. The stories were so darned relatable to her, much more than the usual crud, and she wanted him to know that she identified so naturally with each character despite his normal tendency to skip over major descriptions. It might very well have been the underdog in her, but the list of credentials were what set her over the top.

Sebastian had been modest with his portrayals in such the deliberate way so that the readers could identify his characters more easily either themselves or by the recognition of somebody they had once known or thought of upon the reading. His stories didn't just strike Carrie strongly for her ability to identify with this ambiguity;

the stories themselves paid mostly homage to supporting roles in day-to-day life. His memoir works, though fiction, paid a particular homage to it in their read, and she was rattled by him not expressing his support or his acclaim but only rather soliciting his interest in working with her. Because of this rattle, Sebastian was extremely lucky that Carrie had come to such the pivotal point in her work morale to even consider his offer.

Chapter One:

"Carrie Rutherford,

We writers are so often typecast individuals, of a type whom never tire in the slightest. Our characters are really us on a basic auto-pilot throughout our boring lives, so it would seem to just anybody. You are not just anybody as your work has shown. This blank page stares up as it's being written upon, and is filled without your response having been fully considered – any of it. Because the stereotypes set us the stick-and-move sort of expectations from society, we hide even when walking out in public eyes. Most people tend

to think that we do not ever
seek out friendship, as I am
not doing here. We are homely
looking and seek nothing, in
fact, if you believe these
stereotypes, pet players in
the roles of filthy monsters
having said things so near-
miss to the truth.

As the typecast people we
are, we are responsible only
for living out our lives from
stereotype to stereotype had
at us from the second-classy
society of people whom enjoy
seeing the vision of somebody
else's vision and forget that
somebody out there actually
has sat down with the concept
and pounded out the idea for
some time. We live amongst
these boring people until the
days of our deaths, and the

truth is that we all know the compulsions devised to deal with it all. Tendency nothing however, once it is compared with correspondence, truth is that our compulsions are only coping devices for loneliness and it's just that as anybody else might find, to which we do need friendship. I am not writing you though for your friendship, as was said; I am posing another proposition because of your keen place of understanding all of this.

The irony when one hasn't slept in days is that dreams come to life in so many ways. For that reason, I'm one for as much sleep as can be had. Dreams are only truth poorly disguised, after-all, and so I've enclosed my credentials rather than making some plea over my aspirations during this heavy dream-state, after having been up quite the while writing the potential players of my roles. I shall put it to you bluntly then, lest our paranoia get the better of us.

Whether it is take-home work or take-work home, this will someday make a great story itself. Until then, I'm sending you this fan-mail of sorts with enclosed stories already written, so that you may get a feel for my work. I've seen you on the screen my whole life. You're nearly my age, and you seem to have it together with no trouble steering clear of the news-reels in which so many actors

in the guild find themselves
stuck.

Once again, this isn't
some invitation to romance.
This is rather an invitation
to work collectively on my
next project, starting here
and with this, in the case
that you might enjoy and so
request more work.

My published materials
vary in topic, and this one
indeed opens with fan mail.
I'm writing you and some
others in hopes that you
notice my credentials as the
slightly established author,
and might be interested in
taking on some responsibility
of taking it where it needs
to go. Not that I - as you
see by my résumé - should not
be expected to do the leg-

work myself. It's in fact
already in the process of
being published, and awaits
my approval to move from
literary work on to its film
production, which means it
awaits one of you.

Sincerely,
Sebastian Preston."

Chapter Two:

Sebastian's letter moved Carrie first from her initial reading position in her chair to another, and then another. She put her hand to her chin firmly, as she contemplated the likelihood of the whole thing being the ploy of some obsessive stalker. After-all it's supposed to happen to celebrities constantly, isn't it? It had not particularly happened to Carrie yet – not so intricately – and she saw no reason at first to chance it happening this time.

Carrie was normally one to respond to almost any fan mail with personal dictation, at the least an autographed head-shot, but this sorry excuse for fan-mail reminded her of something else as well. Occasional solicitors' mail would sometimes skip by her agent's office desk, being missed, and would then be passed to hers unbeknownst to her agent. The commercial enterprises usually met her standards anyway if she had the time for them, so she would simply waltz them back to management and say yes before her agent even had the opportunity to read, but this was different. It was almost the opposite. Besides, the pitch was so vague. So some schmuck writes fan mail and what?

Sure, some movie about fan-mail going any direction would play to many fantasies for her fans, and it would certainly be good for her image. The credentials which Sebastian had enclosed were also indeed impressive, but this wasn't solicitation; it was regular fan-mail. Whether to offer her correspondence weighed on her mind heavily for the moment. Wait, who the hell was this asshole?

Chapter Three:

Sebastian had checked his mailbox twice per day for almost a year, and had gotten no responses from any of the celebrities with whom he'd requested correspondence. His social ambiance was somehow different nonetheless, and everywhere he'd been within this past year his confidence had been stronger. Simply having written the letters had certainly changed his attitude for the better.

In his method, he had wanted to make the personal impression on whomever it was that would play his role of the leading lady, which he'd admit was taking for granted their compassion and their professional understanding as well, however socially they might understand. When he went to the mailbox on this particular day – for the first time – expecting bills and junk-mail, there had been nothing whatsoever. When he went the second time in the afternoon though, something stood out amongst the bills and the junk-mail. It was from Carrie Rutherford, whom was indeed one of his correspondence requests.

Of course he hadn't only sent fan mail rapid fire to all of his idols in show business. He had also been keeping correspondence with Cliff, and waiting patiently for just the right production company to express their

interest in him and his
pitches. It was something of
the professional thing to do.

Sebastian indeed worked
professionally as the writer
he claimed to be, and his
credentials were in fact
impressive, even if none of
his works had made it to the
big time as it's called. He'd
written and directed amateur
films of course, which he
produced on his own, but even
for starting out they were
all low budget or no budget
productions. He knew that as
a first timer when it came to
selling his idea to a company
that would pay anything of
value into his work he would
have to start at personal
levels, and initially that
had meant local theater.

He'd gone to every local theater and with every decent pitch he had, but none would take him seriously with only independent films – and low quality ones at that – under his arm. So he drafted some playwrights, except that they only wanted to buy them for their own directors, and for the same meager prices which his film scripts usually sold. So it was right back to Cliff, where he continued to scrape by selling his stories for other directors and their work.

When it came down to it, in the writing business, very few can sell an idea so incidentally to a production company that the company has enough trouble picturing the product to put faith into the same writer's direction.

Selling an idea so little usually indicated that there was never even an idea in the beginning, so the faith which was so important for letting their director — Sebastian — show his idea rather than telling it was what he needed so desperately, and he knew that faith would only ever come on personal levels. So he kept on going to local theaters and made sure he was friendly in his community with the companies to which Cliff could sell his work.

Cliff was pretty good at picturing Sebastian's ideas and selling them as films which turned out nothing like the originals. He knew that if Sebastian could have his work published and read by significant audiences, then the ideas wouldn't have to be changed so much between the authorship and the screening, but in the day in age they lived it was nobody whom wanted to read anything more than what could be found on social-media for free. So Cliff didn't mind whether the idea wasn't changed or was, since he didn't quite get the whole concept of social-media and since Sebastian would constantly express contempt for it. Cliff still got paid, and Sebastian was so darned friendly that the job was fairly easy. The means, by which the two of them made ends meet, in Cliff's frame of reference anyway, could hardly actually be considered scraping. Sure, mostly the work didn't sell for much of anything in its usual case but most all of it sold for something, and certainly was in quite great quantity.

It was a sad truth once the internet was popular that people had always fathomed an ideal that they'd actually finish a book online, and an unfortunate truth that their eyes would always become so distracted if not blinded by the trial of actually trying it. This kept any true fans of Sebastian's from ever discovering the author for the raw material, the ideal nonetheless keeping people from buying hard copies of texts even to read before bed or in hospital waiting rooms or aboard one particularly long flight.

What's even sadder was that people in those days viewed reading as something that was only to be done in waiting rooms or during one particularly long flight just to kill time. Cliff tried his best to understand this when Sebastian would explain it to him, but as a lover of the printed word and because of his line of work, the concept of the common person just couldn't really be related to by either of them no matter how much the other tried to explain it. Oh, Cliff tried his best to understand, but in fact most all of the credits which rolled at the ends of the films for which Cliff and Sebastian were in part responsible, and which the common person was rarely ever bothered to read, those credits are the many people trying their darnedest to be friendly. Those credits were the people trying to relate to an everyday common person, whatever the success.

"Cliff," Sebastian began, this evening. It was his and Cliff's monthly sit down at the coffee shop to discuss how much or how little Cliff could sell Sebastian's work from the previous month, and the new business of what had been written since. "It's been a year since I've done something for myself on my birthday."

"That makes you," Cliff responded, "special?"

"I want to tell you what I did last year, and hoping you won't get jealous about your job..."

"What?" Cliff answered, "Have you been working with another agent? Because I'm still going to get paid, you know, so it doesn't bother me in the slightest!" His eyes darted around the shop.

"Ha, naw," Sebastian told him, "I could never do that." He put his hand to his chin and rested firmly on it, and then he spoke into his long sleeve. "The jig is up, he knows...act casual."

"Then what?" Cliff asked, chuckling a little.

"Sent fan mail out with my credentials - i.e. you and my work - enclosed to my pitch for the most desperate thing I could imagine when it came to the story," Sebastian gasped in one breath.

"Um," started Cliff, his voice a little shaky. "You'll have to explain."

"Fan mail, you know?" beckoned Sebastian. "Personal admiration for some role model..."

"With your pitch for a story attached?"

Sebastian hesitated, "Um, sorta..."

"Um, sorta? What was the story?"

"It begins with fan mail from some run of the mill guy who wants to work with the star he's written..."

"Okay, and...?"

"And nothing, that wasn't even definitively the story idea."

"You're going to have to elaborate..."

"Well," Sebastian turned his head to make sure no one was listening to them, "after my sample of some poetic bullshit, I just wrote that the stars and I begin that way, and left my credentials enclosed."

"So, for your birthday, you wrote out your resume and

some pitch into fan mail to whom?"

"Bunch of people," said Sebastian, clenching his fist around Cliff's napkin, "but here's the clincher...it was a story that you sold..."

"Ooh," Cliff sighed, sitting back in his seat, "fake out..."

"And today I noticed the real clincher...are you ready for this?" Cliff nodded his head, sitting forward again slightly. "One of the people actually responded."

Chapter Four:

"Dear Sebastian,

You caught me in perfect
timing. I'm currently in this
pivotal point in my career
which affords me the ability
responding to fan mail. You
seem really nice, so I should
just tell you right off the
bat that I'm not looking for
any attachments. My friends
are mostly stand-ins, ha. I
normally only send headshot
picture autographs because to
be honest that's all that's
usually requested of me. I'm
really not sure exactly what
your story is (the story to
you *or* the story to your
fiction). I think that your
pitch or your obsession or

whatever it was needs some
professional care, yet your
credentials seem to say that
you've done this before. Has
it worked? I'm not really
sure why I'm responding (or
rambling, for that matter),
all I know is that there are
a great many of key questions
which need answering for my
agent or any agent for that
matter to even consider you.
You suggested that your story
begins with fan mail, but did
you mean that was even a
pitch at all? I may not get
to work on it myself but I
can certainly pass the buzz
along for you. I must say
that I was only interested in
the idea after I did my
homework on you. I like your
work to an extent I suppose.

Assuming you have even part
of the gift necessary to be
discovered and that you're
not representing on someone
else's behalf, in my opinion
you've done the right thing
in reaching out to potential
players as well as the
companies in your resume. In
case you care for my advice
you should keep at sending
your letter to plenty of
players you've in mind for
your roles and even the ones
you don't. Who knows who else
might be interested? As for
myself, I'm grown so tired of
false industry relationships
that poking fun of them in a
mock parody of the irony
you've within the bulk of
your work actually seems fun,
contributing to the industry

45

itself with some relationship started on the basis of the fandom – in the play, mind you, not in real life. I'd likely show it much more interest should the full script come through to my own study, but these things need to be done through the proper channels. I've noticed that most of your stories have twists as they come to a close. Where does your idea take me or any of the other players you may have sent to? Again there are indeed proper channels you must fight to be noticed, unfortunately. Your agent must solicit my agent (only likely to happen after having gone through trusted agents whom may or may not keep it for themselves); I'll

just let you know that now. I
can only assume your player
responds to you, and is it
for an independent work? Is
it some sort of obsession-
suspense story? I'm not sure
how much of your own life
goes into your work, but the
players don't form some bond
creating the story as real
life unfolds do they? Also,
am I playing right into your
idea to get inspirational
guesses to pluck from with
each person you've sent? I'm
no writer myself, really am
rambling aren't I? I've run
my paragraph on so far that
you can surely tell I'm not
the person to help you form
the literary side in any way.
Nor have I any interest in
being some simple muse for

anyone, but am offering my guesses as inquiries because it's true as I've told you that while I've no interest in any attachments, you've caught me in a pivotal point. So I've enclosed some hints amongst my own credentials regarding the best companies to follow. Now knowing them your story might indeed come through my study someday. Finally, I must say your mail was much more interesting than most of what comes through my box. Quite a few people have written what my next piece of work should be, although it's rare to come across somebody with at least a handful of the appropriate credentials. All of the best of luck to you with your success, and one more thing, my reason for writing you has been considered. It's because that pivotal point mentioned now twice. My own work must meet the same points with my work morale itself and the morale has had me trying to get into more independent work. Keep that between us, okay? Well, I'm sorry to say your response is soon coming to an end. Quite the handful, wasn't it?

Sincerely,
Carrie Rutherford.

Chapter Five:

Carrie dropped the letter into the mailbox and rushed on with her errands, as if the world had seen all that she'd done. She didn't much care for the public mailbox. Often the paparazzi lingered, waiting for anything from one easy slip from the blouse to the next full fledged flash. At first she would flip her strongest bird at all of the paparazzi she dealt with in the start of her career, until she realized that they were mostly just the appalled Hollywood tourists as ashamed of what they were doing as she was ashamed of them.
She lived in Hollywood, right in the heart of it all

by choice, as so many players did in wait for the next big thing. She was never really worried when her big breaks would come or even whether they would come at all, and anyway she wasn't home often enough to really care about big pay-offs. The artist in her made sure to remedy any desire for glamour every time a *truly* great script came across her desk, and to her a truly great script was never about the glamour or even the money.

Occasional studio shoots were of course nice. When she was home though – which was indeed rare – most of her time would be in fact spent reading and responding to fan mail. Her house was fairly well kept, only because it was so well avoided. She actually avoided her house so much with her artistic travels that she'd sometimes feel great need to sleep with all of the lights in the house brightly lit, in part warding off any potential intruders, but mostly because the place genuinely seemed haunted. She could talk about it all she wanted, to family, to friends, to therapists, even to her agents when she was desperate for work just to get out of the spookiness, and still no one really fully understood.

Her family was about as supporting of her work as can be expected with some of the material she had produced in her roles. Her friends were practically limited to others in the profession revolving from one project to the next, and even they didn't quite understand just how infamous her entity had become among the underground of film. She knew it could be her own complex, she could admit it, and that she tended to get along better with supporting players and even stand-ins.

Her roles were often full of underdog angst, the type that would sleep around just to do so or in other words reality-based for somebody not worried about her image or reputation by the cynics of the world. Often the story she would read for would go as such, girl meets plenty of boys until special boy comes along. Not that her choice in roles was simplistic in a bad way, or that the type of story for her was ever the uninspired type either; and on the contrary, the type she would play in usually was quite unique. She couldn't be pigeon toed into one genre, and that's why she fit so well into her own underground following. It's also why the cynical type would stoop to criticizing her choices in roles; they didn't have any means by which to categorize her.

Anybody that might be subordinate from job to job would easily receive from her friendly side, so she would usually befriend supporting roles as she herself was often in that line of work. Her relationships outside of work were only really ever tough with those her roles supported, leading players or production designers. She did get along with directors and authors very well because they usually – if they did their jobs correctly – knew her roles to be more on the self-reliant side. So she would schmooze them all she could at parties. In the end though, she got her kicks only ever wanting to play matchmaker with her company. She was always helping people find work and setting up her stand-ins with other players when they needed work. It even went so far that she'd begun setting up stand-ins on dates with old boyfriends, which was the pivotal point in her work morale.

Carrie was done turning over the devoted to something fake, as if it were some test on both ends to old friends' testament. Of course those supporting players – stand-in players – genuinely had their personalities to her, but she was biased when it came to pawning off old boyfriends, and she genuinely missed the guilt to normally associate with female vanity. On the ethical end, helping others to find work had taken its toll on hers and she was ready to be helped herself.

It'd been so long since she worked on a project from

the start. It was true about there being proper channels for any story to go through, and about the very few agents whom would even consider any independent works often being kicked to the bottom of the industry for doing so. Nobody cared to have their leading player in anything besides leading box-office films, to which Carrie had too often noticed herself filling. It was also true that agents will only take material from trusted agents most if not all of the time. It just tends to be too much work to keeping clients away from projects once they've started and especially if the clients are allowed to fill any role they want.

Carrie's particular agent was the type titled talent director, which meant that he chose which work Carrie would take for herself. All of the reasons to be kept from independent films at first had added to the desire in Carrie to work for such an agent – at least for the while it took to establish and to familiarize herself within the business, only she truly *had* tired of the drama involved in all of the phony relationships off the screen that it takes to keep up with box-office expectations. So Sebastian's letter had been one big breath of fresh air for her.

Far beyond being managed, which should not be confused

with having an agent, Carrie was gifted in her childhood and blessed with support from the right people. She could afford to rub elbows with the best of directors within the industry and was fairly well known for taking charge with the directions of the smaller roles. Still, once she was ready to retire from acting, she had very often considered directing, and had begun to consider more and more that maybe it was just a matter of taking her turn at the wheel with some small budget films. Only she couldn't write. She didn't have the first notion of creating an idea or a template or an outline. The stories just didn't come to her.

There wasn't any field to fall back on, as Carrie was a childhood star, and that risk made dipping her feet and rubbing elbows with directors really the extent of her safe options. Because of this she was only the more excitable when stories came lurking around corners or when small opportunities to assist were presented to her. She wasn't just going to let Sebastian slip by.

Chapter Six:

"So which story was it?" Cliff asked.

"It was the one," began Sebastian, "where the girl is slowly driven crazy by the doctors trying to tell her she's only a little bit crazy...you know the one I'm talking about?"

"She finds the good in the crazy?" Cliff inquired, "and then they don't believe her...third person irony and all that sort, that the one?"

"That's the one, 'Living the Dream' it was called..."

"You sent your pitch out to hundreds of celebrities for only one feature length film...and that's the one you chose?"

"Uninspired right?" added Sebastian.

"Don't be hasty there," Cliff consoled, "there are a few positive sides to it, you know..."

"Like what?"

"Well, it normally takes great long whiles to receive any sort of response with fan mail."

"Yeah, but it was lousy and she wants something more substantial to what had been pitched in the letter...she didn't so much as mention the *attached* one..."

"You mean she didn't say anything about '*Living the Dream*' and you're worried?"

"It was still attached, Cliff..."

"Whoever it was responded she might only be the *first,* have you considered that? And by the way I'd just soon not know who it is; I could get in trouble..."

"Is it really that bad?" Sebastian asked, curious.

"You wouldn't believe, the whole agency can be sued for your garnishes if the both of us were in on it together, but the good thing for you is that there's ample headway to be made even if you only get a handful of responses..."

"Buzz and whatnot, yeah, totally...she said she'd pass around the word about me..."

"Sebastian, this is all on the personal level, you can *totally* start a buzz for yourself and in one hell of a genuine way without even ever making the story happen..."

"I enclosed credentials," Sebastian confessed, "could you help out with maybe what to say? Like can you even be endorsed in any way?"

"Out of the question, she can look me up if she wants to, and the whole agency if she's actually interested, but it would be considered far too unethical to say anything personal about it," Cliff explained, "you didn't did you?"

"Naw just a basic resume, the personal letter was about independent stuff..."

"Well hell kid, you've actually managed to hook somebody without any sort of solicitation, and in polite manner where correspondence addresses are open to just that sort of thing. Be polite as can be. If you brought *me* into the thing it'd become straight up harassment...see, you've got the advantage in personal correspondence with this person whoever she is, but for me there are proper channels necessary..."

"That's exactly what she wrote!!" exclaimed Sebastian. "I mean, she wrote that she wants to avoid any sort of attachments, and she asked what the full story was, and that was just about the skinny..."

"So then only tell her the story..."

"You already sold the story..."

"What, you're afraid of being rude? She waited a year to respond..."

"Just, I don't want to take the only chance I might have telling her that we need to start from square one, you know?"

"Tell her what happened with the story and then maybe throw another idea into the same letter while you're at it..."

"Pitch another whole idea after explaining how the other story did?"

"Well," Cliff added, "she asked, didn't she?"

"Okay," Sebastian said "well then, she only said that she'd need to know more in order to be interested, sort of hypothetically, so I guess she didn't ask for anything but the story in question..."

"So *she* actually drew *you* into the whole thing becoming a now professional discussion did she?"

"That's sort of what was intended with my letter in the first place, bud," said Sebastian condescendingly.

"It's most definitely," concluded Cliff, "her method of clinching you then."

"Um...what?"

"Proper channels, if you cannot keep correspondence to the personal level, and she explicitly expressed that she wished against the personal level relationship right?"

"Yeah..."

"Well, there are proper channels that must be taken before professional talk..."

"So, what? I'm shit out of luck? They're all probably trained to be that way."

"Hold up, now, you've got your options left."

"Which are?"

"You can give it a bit for the buzz to circulate, maybe just wait in case you receive correspondence from others..."

"Okay...?"

"Maybe by then the story will have come across them and they'll have heard of you already. Your stories do get turned down by quite the big channels sometimes, I'll tell you that much..."

"So then they'll know I'm failing miserably?"

"Hey now, I'm in that boat too you know, they'll know you're struggling...that means you're still genuine, and your luck's better with genuine, right?"

"Are there any other options?" Cliff's idea to do nothing was quite far from impressive.

"Right," Cliff told him, "you don't send the story's information save for how well it did."

"Dude," Sebastian grunted while dropping his head to his hands, "they didn't even use it, it was a flop..."

"Dude," Cliff mocked him, "it was a sale."

Chapter Seven:

"Carrie Rutherford,

I'm so glad you took the time to respond, I'm fairly sure most of what you wrote was flattery and to say the least. Run-on paragraphs have never bothered me any. You'd written that in order to be interested should the story come through your study you'd need to know more of what it was about. I'm afraid that that particular story has actually already been made. I'll admit that it flopped horribly, wasn't even used, but it sold at any rate. Perhaps you'd be interested in other stories from this year. Actually, my latest has been inspired by what you wrote about yourself, and it wouldn't go with my morals to make it without you or at least your blessing. I'm in all hopes for that *not* coming off as obsessive, I only feel like I owe you one now. Maybe your junction will allow you the time needed, and maybe you yourself could use some support. I know I certainly could. Nothing attached this time. What am I offering you? I'm not really sure. It's in your court.

Sincerely,
Sebastian Preston."

Chapter Eight:

Carrie kept on dragging through the business of her day after having dropped her correspondence to Sebastian. She had kept the mailbox in her mind all the night prior for the first task of her morning, since farthest from her home that she'd planned to travel all day.

She was meeting one of her many stand-in friends at the coffee shop to drop off her usual grocery list. This particular friend, Loraine, ran errands as a job for several people around the area, although the special relationship between Carrie and herself was in having worked together on some of the actual film projects of Carrie's.

Lorraine did not quite resemble Carrie as much as the stand-ins whom would be sent for something big like the nice thanksgiving dinner prank. Her hair wasn't the right texture. Her nose was, to put it gently, less glamorous. She was also some inches shorter than Carrie. The one thing that kept the two working together was that proportional difference only the two of them shared, which is they shared the rump of the same goddess.

Carrie frequently chose Lorraine for the groceries task because of that specific display of rump that only pivoting the large shopping carts could handle, and when Lorraine would dip over the steering bar to step onto the bottom basket and reach those cans of peaches on the second from top shelf, every passer by would reminisce of that first feature, particular to each, to which Lorraine's jumped out at them, of course pairing their fandom to Carrie.

Carrie smiled at this as she approached the coffee shop, when Lorraine stood from her table to greet her. The man whom had been sitting across from Lorraine also rose. Carrie shot him one cocked brow, her other brow cocked to Lorraine.

"Carrie," yelled Lorraine as she jumped from her chair,

"so good as always to see you, simply you must meet Charlie..." She held her arms to the man, Charlie, as he was approaching.

"That'd be me," laughed Charlie, "you look different than expected."

"Well," Carrie started, uneasily. "I'm the better looking one, ha." She cranked her head to Lorraine and whispered. "Who's Charlie?"

"Charlie's new," answered Lorraine, "we've been seeing each other awhile and thought it was time he met one of my bosses."

"You seemed to be the most interesting," spouted Charlie, "from the most of Lorraine's stories."

"We wanted to surprise you," added Lorraine.

"Well, you can be," spoke Carrie, "certain that it's a mission accomplished." There was some shake in her voice, "shall we sit?"

"Sure," said Charlie, "we saved your seat." The three sat as Carrie took her first sip of the coffee she'd trusted hers.

"So, down to business then," Lorraine said proudly, "Charlie wants to see me in action."

"Oh," Carrie spat, nearly losing her lip to her coffee, "well today's list is pretty small, just the essentials. I am out of peaches though." She glanced at Charlie. "So how long have the two of you actually been together?"

"Couple months," answered Lorraine, "not long..." This time Carrie actually did lose her lip to the coffee. She had to take the cup slowly and with two hands to recover it. "Really," Lorraine added, "only long enough to trust him knowing what my job really is with you..."

"Tell me then," Carrie demanded, more than somewhat shrewdly of Charlie, setting down her coffee. "Tell me that you like her for more than my ass." Lorraine was popping at her knuckles while Charlie laughed.

Chapter Nine:

Sebastian sat in his home contemplating his next story. While he knew that it just would not be right to make it into anything without the blessing from Carrie, even if he had to contact her agency with his own pitch expressing his interest in Carrie acting the role. Made into anything or not, he would make sure it got to her. After-all, he had given his word - in a way - when he wrote her that she'd inspired it in him. He felt he was growing obsessive, but he'd spoken too soon and so it was the right thing to do.

It was going to require requesting agency agreements in writing that the script would fall into her hands. Last resort, he thought. She might just respond again. For all he knew she'd even request it personally, but truth be told he really didn't know. So for now it was time to write the thing, and he would worry about the desperation resorts later.

He did know that it would for the time being be sufficient to simply go ahead and send her the script through the same medium in which he'd promised it to her and hope that she wrote back again. So he thought it over and concluded that it was unlikely for some form of legal restraint on his right to do just that, even if *this* might be what would tip the odd ends to stir. As long as he knew she received it, and that the buzz would be going around about him and his writing, the ends would justify the means as far as his favor was concerned. He felt that he should regret promising her his next piece of writing in the way that he did, or at least that he should feel guilty about using her to further his own reputation, but the more he thought it over the more he realized it had likely been all he could've said to keep her corresponding with him. She had trapped him after-all.

For the moment he knew he needed to start the story if he was ever going to start it. If she responded to him, then great, and if not he'd send it along and forget the ordeal just like he had the last time. His pen scratched the pages fantastically as he sipped rapidly at his coffee with all new and unexpected twists. When he was inspired, his writing surprised even him.

Some four chapters into it the time came to prepare dinner for himself. Some nine chapters in, it was time to fall into his bed where he would toss for some three hours before his first dream. He'd had one of those dreams where one tosses and turns all the more than in falling asleep in the first place, making it hard to tell if he ever even fell asleep at all, only to awaken late in the morning hours fully rested.

When he awoke from that continuous stir quite past his normal awaking hour, rare for someone like Sebastian, his pen scratched yet again. Recalling dreams from years before, he jotted brainstorms and outlines for the next few stories before it was time for lunch, having missed any decency in eating breakfast. Around noon he had eaten his lunch completely and was back to the story. By four passed noon his daily mail had come, bills and junk-mail.

Sebastian was writing for his own self, from beginning to end. He'd simply promised the idea and its premise to

Ms. Rutherford. It indeed was right to send her copy along and to leave it between them, as thanks to her for having taken the time to send her heartfelt correspondence even if it had only been to express non interest for his original proposition. Should she know and understand that people change, then she would surely know that she herself might change her mind in case she hadn't been interested in working with him at all, and not just because she didn't know the full story. Even if she'd just been being polite, that is, her mind might change for ample reasons and there would be no reason to get upset at just one more

letter. So he gave her until
the work was finished.

Two weeks into the story
Ms. Rutherford did show that
she understood. Sebastian had
received her response from
his last bit of mail – the
one about writing his next
story for her – along with a
pile of junk-mail, no bills
though. He'd decided not to
tell Cliff about this one,
not wanting to get his agent
or himself into unnecessary
trouble. Besides, this was
Sebastian's big break to keep
things personal with somebody
in the industry and he felt
that he might be tempted to
speak business if he went any
further speaking with Cliff
for advice.

Sebastian would of course continue to write his piece for Ms. Rutherford, and then after considering what she thought of and wanted from the work he'd decide later whether or not he should show it for sale. She certainly would have different position about critique, not only for her investments being made unique.

When Sebastian considered the words of Ms. Rutherford he understood all that to have been her wish anyway. If the story was for her then it should be up to her what is done with it. She also had her different positions in the industry. Sebastian just saw it as courtesy to keep her in the loop, but still couldn't help thinking about the buzz and feeling proud and guilty at the same time. It's true he'd obsessed, but he knew that perhaps she might only be interested in his other works and even in soliciting for him if he did this just right, but he also knew that doing it just right meant being genuine and not letting things get that far ahead. This meant he'd have to be genuinely honest.

He was thinking business already and needed to avoid that. So he pressed forward with the story, affording her latest thoughts into his and letting his thoughts sink.

Chapter Ten:

"Dear Sebastian,

I'm sorry to hear about
your story as it was. Did you
ever find the right person
for the role? What's really
important is whether you were
and are happy with it. It
doesn't matter if it was a
success or even that it sold.
My word, you really want to
write another just for me?
Whom was the other one for?
Upon reflection it does seem
much. Although you were right
about my morale perhaps
needing support and you're
especially right to recognize
your own need for support, it
could be then that we never
need to be involved as they

say in order to offer that special support you certainly want. I'll be honest; I'm truly worried whether you're the trustworthy type. You've already distracted me from work, although as I told you I was sort of searching for the distraction. We have no need to talk business because it would be shameful of me to lead you down a road I myself don't trust, but for me to simply be your critic I think I might be able to read the new story you had in mind. I'm very interested to know what in my previous letter sparked this new story within you though first. I'm not sure just anyone should know about the secret that I'd written and would appreciate you sending it for my thoughts before you run with it as they say. You seem to have me pinned here. Of course do not use my name. I'm actually very worried about it all. Can you tell? Guess if I'm to be only the censor, you may as well not know much more about my personal aspirations. Suffice to say, if you really do care to support me in turn, you can always just send it along so I'll know what I'm getting into. It would not only take away my fears, it would ease me through into that pivotal change in my career that was mentioned. Of course while my own goals were to write and direct and produce some things myself, your idea

might be just the right start
for you and I wouldn't want
to steal that. I know I just
contradicted my desire not to
tell you much more about
myself business-wise but you
do have me pinned don't you?
Are you noticing my concern
and excitement to read at
once? I haven't even seen the
original story but I suppose
whatever you want to send is
up to you. You'll have my
correspondence attention for
about two weeks I'd say.

Sincerely,
Carrie Rutherford."

Chapter Eleven:

Sebastian immediately had thought he knew what to make of Ms. Rutherford's response. She had actually requested only two things technically, which were for him to send the story and for him to send more explanation about it, by default asking of him exactly what he'd planned to do at the story's end, which meant he needed to finish quick.

He wasn't quite sure how it should end, and so he wasn't quite sure to what it should lead. He was up to her third audition with stand-ins. So far within the story, her character had accepted anyone and everyone for any and every role to which they auditioned so long as each audition had resembled her in even just slight ways. It didn't even matter to her character whether the other characters looked like her, it only mattered that they held themselves well. Her character was even sort of comedic in her assumptions that people with the same stubborn attitude would have the same work morale as the casting lead within the story.

In the real world and in the meantime, Carrie all the way across the country had been conjuring her own piece of fiction. The two wrote their respective works with their respective nightfalls and with their own respective frantic races against the deadline.

Sebastian's story was of some insecure woman casting whom she saw as more alluring women simply because their eyes or their hair or their bust met her criteria. These women would all inevitably need to be replaced at the casting director's wishes, no matter what the casting lead demanded. Some would miss at the necessary charisma and some would have over-whelming stage fright. Some were over-acting atrociously and others didn't agree with the roles enough for which they'd signed on to play. One thing they all had in common was taking with them important contributors to the project because of love interest. One took the entire grip team and production had to be delayed. Another sparked a spontaneous protest among some supporting players when she was fired and the one left with her, causing production to again be delayed.

It was turning into quite the fiasco in Sebastian's fiction and he was afraid that he might be stepping on some toes should he turn Ms. Rutherford's character into a jealous control freak. He certainly did not want to guess at her sense of humor, and so he hadn't found any ending suitable for all of the guesswork. Then it hit him. He could take advantage of his own vulnerability by changing her character into his own self. She could be the innocent producer whose play keeps getting delayed. It was genuine and it was honest, being in sort of that position as he was. His first draft wouldn't take too long after-all. In fact, he was almost done.

He wrote up a mock draft with a quick ending in which the play within the story folded into itself as the feature characters in the work were making it, and the producer's story became the film that was being made by those producers among whom he'd written Ms. Rutherford's role. He could include some author's notes and send the whole thing right along, and so he wrapped up the story and did just that.

His author's notes were thankful of her consideration and time and his basic hopes that she would like what he'd made. He made no more offers, as it had already been the whole month without anything to show to Cliff besides brainstorms, the whole month in waste if Ms. Rutherford *wasn't* going to like it.

For those whom wonder, Carrie's own literature was not even quite literature but only outline and actually just being completed on paper as the letter from Sebastian reached her fan mail box. In her play her character was playing matchmaker with her circle of friends, composed of previous stand-ins. She didn't consider her story to show much integrity, having not conceived of hardly any actual fiction as of yet. She did at least discover that she had been playing that role all along in real life, and she actually thought of her own ending. Until then she had only discouraged herself with the whole task. She'd merely been trying to guess what it was Sebastian had to work with, and her ending really tied it all together.

After having set matches for her circle of stand-in friends, her character became very jealous of always being the maid of honor with each

consequential wedding. In her
story there were surprisingly
quite the lot of similarities
to Sebastian's story in their
comedic natures and in that
the humor throughout was only
handfuls of the running jokes
about the look-alike topic.
In the end her character had
met some wedding crasher at
one of the receptions who'd
happened to do stand-in work.
He explained it to her
finally that stand-ins don't
have it any easier than the
glamour stars. All the glory
without the glamour doesn't
actually come with much
glory. It actually draws the
wrong kinds of attention, and
it must be some friend to
have set up the arrangements
for them, famous or not. The

outline had closed with some
joking ideas between the two,
and as soon as she read
through her work Carrie knew
she ought to make it into
something. It wasn't her
first work, only the first
she thought could become any
sort of feature. If it was
only the main title in some
book of short stories, it
could actually someday have
become something and she knew
it, being at the pivotal
point where she was in work
morale. Among all the other
people she'd show, for some
reason, she wanted to send it
to Sebastian, wondering what
he'd written or if he hadn't
finished yet or if he was
even writing at all.

She considered how her
agent might respond to it if
she were to tell him that
she'd written something. Most
likely he would be angered
that she was wasting time
with independent work and he
wouldn't want to have any
part of it.

She considered that maybe
Sebastian's agent would be
interested. If she could only
turn the tables on Sebastian
in some sort of trade between
their connections, it was
hard to find an agent so low
in the industry who would
actually work on independent
literature. If the agent
wasn't going to be interested
maybe at the least Sebastian
had some smaller industry
connections within his other

channels. The trade could be for other work of hers if he was willing to be patient, and any day her acting gigs might start up again. She really didn't want to end her little sabbatical as she was rather enjoying her pivots as well as her fan-mail, and especially her new story.

All Carrie knew was that she didn't want to shuffle into some big wig's office as one of the clumsy dime-a-dozen writer wannabes that they get all too often, at least not if she could get potential references before all that had to be done. First she confirmed further correspondence with Sebastian to be in her better interest, and staring up at the sealed envelope containing his last letter, which she'd propped upon her writing desk, she made the decision to open and read.

She could hardly contain herself and immediately wrote her response, this time proud to drop it in the public mailbox. She was so giddy she almost even shopped all by herself – almost.

Chapter Twelve:

"Dear Sebastian,

It was of great pleasure to read your work, and I'm glad you've sent it. You do indeed have some gift in you, and I'm actually not afraid to admit that it was easy to identify with your character. In real life I really am sort of snobby when it comes to my stand-ins, and it's in quite legitimate fear that any one of them might hog the screen, often sizing them up with the one feature which resembles me. I'm glad that you made it comedic. The real irony that struck me in your work was the greatest fear I've of my stand-ins derailing some of

the production with *their* own
egos. It rarely occurs where
people let the idea go so to
their heads that there needs
to be a delay to the
production, but the fear of
it is always close to my
heart because I really don't
get the opportunity to get to
know many of them as I rarely
have much control over the
casting. The casting director
might normally audition the
stand-ins, and the leads only
get so many opportunities to
meet them. It's such a short
opportunity that sometimes I
only get to meet with them at
the last minute, where-in it
really is like checking them
good to fit into my shoes –
so to speak. Much of the time
stand-ins are needed is in

post production, because they are mostly used to fill in gaps which may be re-shot while the actual lead players are already working in other productions. So when I do get the opportunities to meet my own stand-ins I make sure to take full advantage. Some of them have worked with me in more than one feature because of referrals. It might be only because it's out of my want for control that I go the extra distance to take care of the people who work with me, but it is usually left to the casting director and out of the producer's hair, and so maybe your story would make more sense if the main plot was around the piece being an independent work. Producers tend to want everything done by the book, but an independent film *about* stand-ins would likely foot the bill more easily so far as casting stand-in players than would most executives. Producers don't trust new players normally. Maybe the producer in the story isn't yet paying for anything and just overseeing the whole plot. If you make sure to specifically mention that part, the piece would be more believable in the whole, and the repetition of set-backs could still take place comically and swiftly. In the end, the director could still find plenty of reasons to cast all too many not so look-alikes if that's what

you were going for. Not sure
if you were actually aiming
for the same value I had read
when all of the cast and crew
members kept quitting because
of romances with the stand-
ins. My take in picturing it
was quite comedic in tragedy.
In my *own* experience with
such the problem, it's always
hard to accept and support a
relation in the workplace,
even if relations are just
brought onto the set to view.
Let alone quitting over the
sort of thing, it's always a
distraction and especially if
the relationship is between
workers of the *same* project
then you've really added
depth to the idea of the
whole concept. I never would
have guessed you'd get your

story from my telling you
that I'm friends with people
in that line of work. It's a
big smack in the face at
workplace relationships from
every side of the circle.
Everybody loses in your story
due to the problem, except
for the sort of eagle-eye
that brings it all together.
It's very rare that fan-mail
stories strike my attention,
you are indeed very lucky. I
hope you know this. Reading
back over all I've written I
realize I'm gushing, and I'm
supposed to be your critic.
At any rate, you'd inspired
me to write my own story to
which an outline has been
enclosed for you. Maybe if we
blend the two you could put
in a good word for me with

your agent. I'm trying to get into independent work which was that pivot I told you about. Maybe your character meets my supporting character during the production of the adapted feature. Your ending would remain except my ending would blend and the character would put it into perspective about the snobby side of things. Viewers like things wrapped up neatly as far as I can tell. Now, however, comes the time when my ego takes control. I'd really like to just take your story from you and do all this myself, but like I said about that whole independent work bit, I'm still pivoting. It's just that if I'm going to change it around you might as well

know that fan mail is hardly
an extended contract, and I'm
asking for your permission to
change the story around a bit
and use it myself. You can
also request payment. Really,
your story is *really* that
good. Maybe it's just because
I've wanted to do something
like this for such a long
time now and also that my
time is available at the
moment. Of course you'd be
getting buzz in the industry
which was my highest hope
regarding your reason for
corresponding in the first
place, but it wouldn't be
fair limiting it just to
that. Blending the stories is
my favorite idea. So we come
to that pivotal point where
your story is yours even with

suggestions from me and my story is mine including the ending. I'm sure you know how copyrights work. If you want to sell then I'll blend the two into film production. I'll only sit on my story so long by itself. Remember this as me saying that I wouldn't work with you, only because of the way that we met. Weigh your options, find what you might make selling your story to somebody else, and keep me informed to make an offer if you please. Or perhaps, and this is where I become coy, you'll want both stories separately for your people. Well, that's everything. Gir.

Sincerely,
Carrie Rutherford."

Chapter Thirteen:

Sebastian was busting for what he'd read. He'd hit the jackpot. Not only had Carrie appreciated his work, she had offered to publish it herself if need be. Of course, all options considered it was the best one possible. The most obvious choice the more he considered it. Ms. Rutherford would likely offer way better finances than his agent would ever have been able to find. The only problem was that Ms. Rutherford had left her offer for Sebastian to decide and hadn't made one of her own. Sebastian would have to either name his own price or he'd have to settle for the option of buying *her* work, which he knew he couldn't afford.

The latter option scared the pants off him since he had never turned down a sale, and he also wasn't about to give her some price just above what Cliff might get considering what she could likely afford. That is to say both options were extremely embarrassing. So he wrote a few of his own questions.

He was sure that he was interested with collaboration of the two stories, and he also wanted to suggest that he had considered his other options before choosing her. This way he could ask her what kind of budget she might have for the production and she might just tell him what she's willing to pay and make her offer.

Sebastian decided that he ought to sleep on the idea, and then again, and his head grew little by little in the coming days. It was just too perfect. Ms. Rutherford was already apparently on better terms with her old stand-ins than most people, he could tell by the way she'd gloated about it. He thought of those roles. His head grew more. She was offering to put the production on herself or with friends of hers or whatever. His head grew still and was about to explode when he re-read the last of her letter. She actually wanted him to write again.

He couldn't wait any longer just pacing his home and gasping in awe. He had to respond for her before doing anything else, and to word it perfectly he needed to feel like he *deserved* the lot of money for it. So he let his head get a little bigger, but by the time he was writing he didn't wind up asking any questions at all. His head shrunk back to normal size as he saw what all was really unfolding, and his thoughts grew more realistic.

Chapter Fourteen:

"Carrie Rutherford,

I'm so glad that you're interested in putting our work into production. Yes, it would be very fitting to add your ending to my story, and even to blend the rest of your work into the rest of mine as sort of its offset. It does make sense that the character should be producing an independent work. Before letting you publish it, for my fee of course, there are some notes of my own that are going to need to be made known. First, yes, it would be your story, save for the co-authorship. I've only ever collected fees to let others

publish my work, and so I'm
very familiar with the way it
works with changes. Now is
indeed the time to brag. Not
to come off narcissistic,
it's just that you need to
know you're not my big break
or anything. This won't add
or take away anything from my
reputation, which has always
counted on one publisher or
another at a time, so please
don't worry about that. I'm
not going to lie about your
fame going a little to my
head, but if you truly don't
have experience in directing,
then please don't worry about
my reputation. I want to
support you. It seems like
too many peas in the pod for
me to try and tell you how as
I've no directing experience

either. I'm interested in a one-time payment and simply to split authorship credits for the royalties that may come. Maybe the title needs some work, what do you think? I like *'Stand-In Room Only.'* Just know I'm on board for the easiest method accepting that I'm asking your offer be quick. The less agents to see it before transferring it to you the better, so I haven't shopped around yet as they say. It is also a time-sensitive matter though, so you know. Trusting that you can afford me, I'm very much looking forward to your next response.

Sincerely,
Sebastian Preston."

Chapter Fifteen:

Carrie wrote Sebastian an immediate offer very formally and thanked him in the post script of her letter. He of course accepted her agreement to transfer the copyright under provision and as soon as Carrie's check came and was cleared the story was hers to do with what she wished. She even added that she would provide credit that the bulk of the story had been conceived by him, and within the coming months the feature film was released. The making of the work made one great story for all of the talk shows on which Carrie appeared to promote it.

"So then what became of the original fiction about the fan-mail?" people would ask. Carrie did her best to promote Sebastian's flop at that question. She did even better though promoting their book of short stories, *"Too Many Peas in a Pod,"* which was released within the same calendar year of *"Stand-In Room Only."* The book of short stories was comprised of work the two of them had continued to share through fan-mail. When they finally met face-to-face at the first book signing either had ever done, Carrie could have sworn that she recognized Sebastian from elsewhere, but she couldn't put her finger on it. The two have remained uninvolved with

one another romantically to
this day.

Epilogue:

"Dear Carrie,

Your story is intriguing to me how your main character learns the lesson that she can't judge the work morale of her coworkers based on how they display their desire to work. If you hadn't told me your own morale had been recently pivotal it'd never have occurred to me that it'd come from personal conflict. Your own experience doesn't show through in the work, it just provides the moral of the story which to me was that anybody can want to work regardless of deserving the work, and also that it really takes tons of trust to weed out who merely wants it from those whom do deserve it. In all hopes you've found that someone like me deserves your best and also that you deserve my best just as I've learned that from your very first letter until now. You haven't lost any of the trust that's been built and my hope is that mine of yours hasn't been anything but built upon as well. The story is yours as your check has cleared, with which to do whatever you wish and my next propositions for the two of us if you're interested include collecting short fiction together. You can hone your craft with such work, trust me. The one story was already good enough for my standards, and it can all

be done through any time
period as we both might need.
It seems quite the profitable
approach for the both of us.
Your promotion for my work in
the beginning about the fan-
mail story has been truly
great for both yours and mine
when it comes to an honest
reputation of integrity. This
next idea seems right, and we
wouldn't have to actually
meet face-to-face to do it,
nor would we have to share
any personal information. It
could be done just the same
as the first project, except
that it would be co-owned
from the beginning this time.
You could also make films out
of them in the coming years.
Send me back if you would
like, once you've finished

promoting the film, no rush
of course. In either case,
I'm so glad you gave my work
the opportunity to reach more
people. Thank you so much for
that.

Sincerely,
Sebastian Preston."

The end.

Proof

Made in the USA
Columbia, SC
20 July 2017